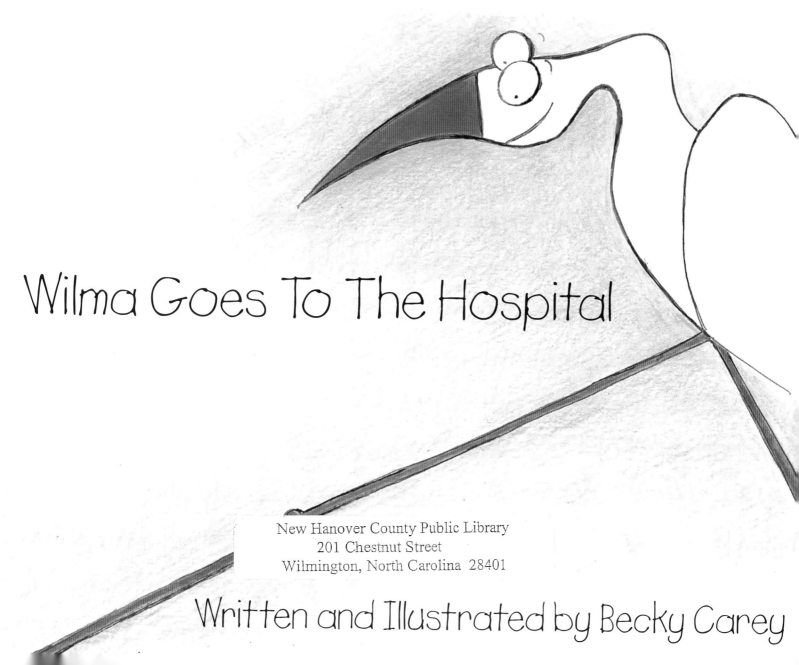

Wilma Goes To The Hospital

Written and Illustrated by Becky Carey

Text and illustrations copyright © 2007 by Becky Carey

All rights reserved, including the right of reproduction in whole or part in any form.

Book design by Becky Carey and Mark Joseph Kelly

The text of this book is set in Lemonade.
The illustrations are rendered in colored pencil and pen and ink on paper.

Printed in USA
Mississippi Printing Company, Inc.

First U.S. edition 2007

Library of Congress, 2007
Cataloging-in Publication Data is available

ISBN 0-9791331-0-6
Printed in USA

MJK Management
Delmar, NY

Wilma's World®

For all the children of the world.

And to

Susan F. Roscher for her valiant heart and her unprecedented belief in me.

Erin and Kate

Today is one of our biggest soccer games, I'm so excited!

Uh oh!

Boing... Boing... OWWWWWW!

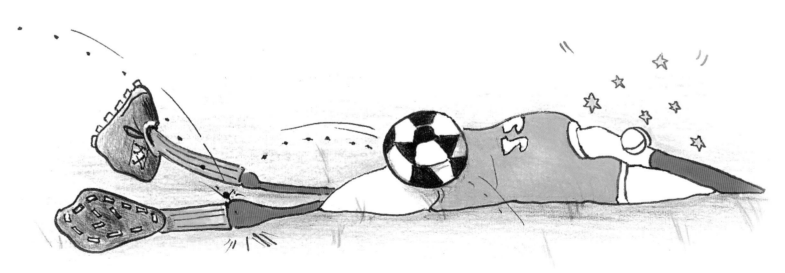

Whoa...
this is my
first time in
an ambulance

Wheeeeeee!
This is kinda cool.

Yikes, it's dark and noisy
but it doesn't hurt

My heart is BIG
and strong and healthy

UH OH, it looks like my leg bone is sorta broken! That's why it hurts!

In we go...
to let the
doctor fix it.

I didn't feel a thing.

"Wilma, can we sign your cast?"

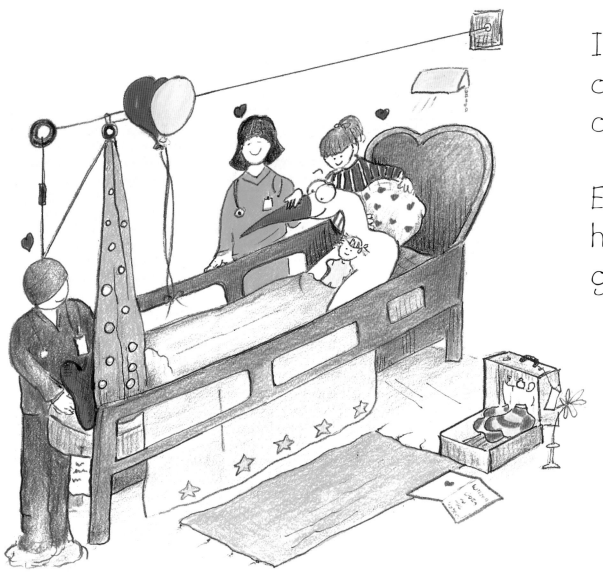

I love my
doctors
and nurses.

Everyone
here is so
good to me

Home Sweet Home

I can't wait to play soccer again!

It's All Good!

My Name

My Doctor

My Favorite Nurse

My Accident

Hospital

Friends

Day I Get to Go Home

Picture of Me

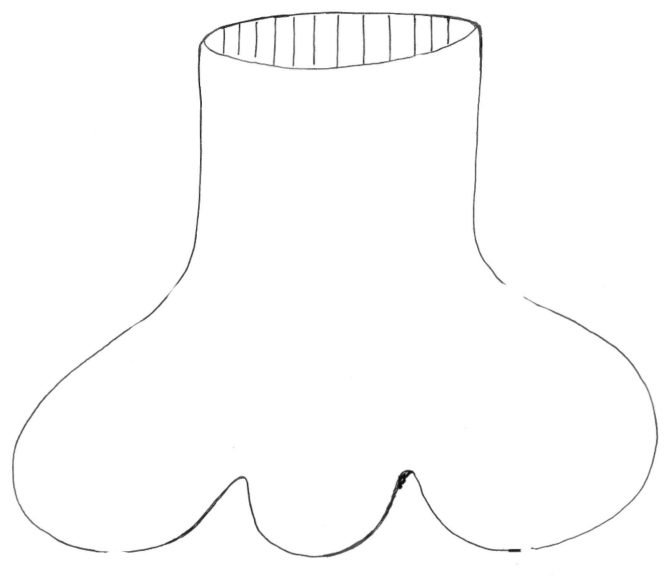

Sign My Cast

ML   2-13